ONE ROOM SCHOOL

AUTHOR'S NOTE AND ACKNOWLEDGMENTS

District records show that students from School 14 first enrolled in Honeoye Falls Central School in September 1945, so the one room school of this book closed in June 1945. This memoir of the school's final year includes at least one event, the great blizzard, that may have occurred in an earlier year. Extensive research by author and illustrator did not always lead to photographs of the specific places and things in the book, and so we used period references instead; for example, the bookmobile is not the same model as the one that visited the school, and the patterns on Miss Shackelton's dresses are based on clothing catalogs from the mid-1940's. In both events and physical details, *One Room School* presents memories of several students, and help from others as well. I am especially grateful to Lucille (Palmer) Pattison, Byron Palmer, Gary Pringle, and Layna (Helen Hutchinson) McCabe. Other students who helped were Eileen (Hutchinson) Havens, Bob McCombs, and Patricia (Cutt) Bennett. Former teachers Phyllis MacNamara, Ethel Anderson, and Beatrice Shackelton (sister of Gladys, the school's final teacher) also provided some details. Finally, I also want to thank Alison (Gifford) Costello, Susanne Geen, present owner of the house that encloses the one room school structure, and Diane Ham, the town historian of Mendon, New York.

—Laurence Pringle

ILLUSTRATOR'S NOTE

The illustrations are collagraphs, literally collage-graphics. For each illustration, many pieces of paper were glued in layers on a piece of heavy cardboard and brushed with gesso and acrylic gel. Each plate was inked, wiped, and printed by hand on an etching press. When dry, each image was colored by hand with watercolor washes and colored pencils.

—Barbara Garrison

ONE ROOM SCHOOL

by Laurence Pringle ◆ Illustrated by Barbara Garrison

Boyds Mills Press

For Gladys Shackelton, Beatrice Shackelton, Phyllis MacNamara,
Ethel Anderson, and all the others who taught in one room schools.—L. P.

For Thea, a true friend of the arts and of artists of all ages.—B. G.

Published by Caroline House
Boyds Mills Press, Inc.
A Highlights Company
815 Church Street
Honesdale, Pennsylvania 18431
Printed in Hong Kong

Publisher Cataloging–in–Publication Data
Pringle, Laurence.
One room school / by Laurence Pringle; illustrated by Barbara Garrison.—1st.ed.
[32] p.: col. ill.; cm.
Summary: A look back at events and the changing of the season at a one-room school
in rural New York during the last year of the Second World War.
ISBN 1–56397–583–1
1. New York (State)—Social life and customs—Juvenile literature.
2. Educational change—United States—History—20th century—Juvenile literature.
[1. New York (State)—Social life and customs. 2. Educational change—United States—
History—20th century—Juvenile literature.] I. Garrison, Barbara, ill. II. Title.
371'.00974—dc20 1998 AC CIP
Library of Congress Catalog Card Number 96–84154

First edition, 1998
Book designed by Rosanne Kakos-Main
Edited by Harold D. Underdown
The text of this book is set in 15 point Stone Serif
The illustrations are collagraph prints.

10 9 8 7 6 5 4 3 2 1

On a warm September morning my brother Gary and I set
out for the first day of school. Every day we walked more
than three miles to and from school—past farmhouses,
barns, pastures, and cornfields.

Our school stood on flat land, surrounded on three sides by cow pasture. It was plain and small, with one classroom and one teacher. It had no name, just a number—14. In 1944 eighteen students came to School 14, in grades one through eight.

Some of the older kids rode bicycles until the winter snows came. Our teacher, Miss Gladys Shackelton, drove to school in her Model A Ford. Once in a while she would give a few of us a ride after school. It was a treat to be whisked home in a car. If the day was warm, we could ride in the rumble seat. The wind blew our hair wildly and almost took my breath away.

The school day began when Miss Shackelton rang the hand bell, calling everybody in. The classes were small. Mine was the biggest by far with five pupils. Helen Hutchinson usually had no classmates at all. When she was in third grade, she was the entire third grade. Then she was the fourth grade, and fifth grade, and so on.

Miss Shackelton had wavy auburn hair. She often wore dresses made with a flower pattern, and dusty rose nail polish. When she came close to my desk, I could smell her perfume. A girl said it was called Tabu.

Miss Shackelton taught us all to read and write and multiply.
She taught us the history of New York State, where we lived,
and about the war that troubled the whole world at the time.

Sharper in my memory are the stories she told about big snapping turtles that lived in a pond by her house and about a woodchuck she had tamed. She showed us snapshots of the woodchuck, scratching at her screen door for treats. It ate ice cream!

Miss Shackelton began each day by giving older students a reading assignment or other work. While they worked quietly, she gave lessons to the early grades. Then the young ones worked while the upper grades were taught.

Sometimes, I covered my ears to shut out the voices of the other kids and Miss Shackelton. Sometimes, though, I enjoyed listening to lessons of the other grades.

Older boys and girls helped younger ones learn to spell or to multiply. And Miss Shackelton often brought several grades together for a common lesson. Right after lunch she usually read a story to all eight grades. That fall she read a long book, day by day, about a girl who had been captured and raised by Indians. I liked the story so much that I felt sad when it ended.

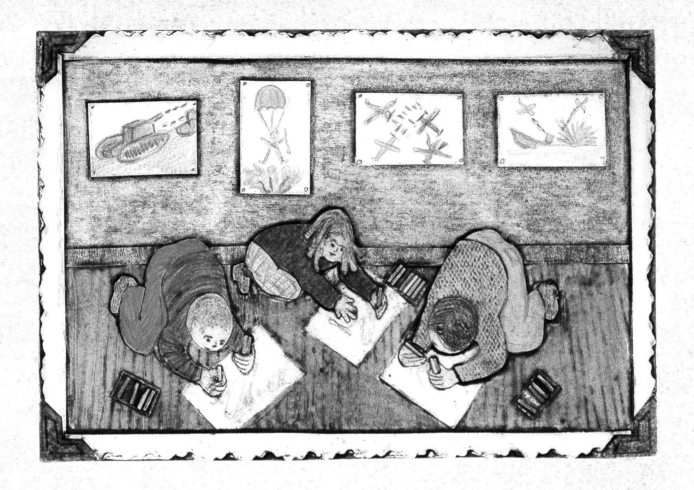

We often played war, fighting imaginary enemies at recess. The schoolyard rang with boys' voices imitating the sounds of rifles, machine guns, and exploding grenades. Girls pretended to be nurses, caring for the wounded soldiers.

During free time indoors, both boys and girls often drew scenes of tank battles and dogfights between airplanes. We knew all the details of P–51 Mustangs, P-38 Lightnings, and B–17 Flying Fortresses.

As the autumn days grew chilly, we wore coats to school and hung them in the cloakroom. The cloakroom had another use, too. There, with the door closed, Miss Shackelton could talk to students privately—or punish them.

Once at recess I threw gravel at some girls. Miss Shackelton took me to the cloakroom and told me to hold out my hand, palm up. She hit my hand with a ruler. *Whack, whack, whack!*

It hurt but I tried not to cry. *Whack!* Nothing could be worse, I felt, than having the other kids see that I had cried. *Whack, whack!* Then I saw that Miss Shackelton herself seemed about to cry. Tears flooded my eyes. The punishment stopped.

One autumn afternoon Miss Schackelton took us on an unusual hike. We walked along roadsides, stuffing milkweed seedpods into empty onion bags. The fluffy parts of the seeds were used in life preservers to keep sailors afloat when their ships sank in battles at sea.

That fall we also gathered scrap iron from our homes and from our neighbors. Eighth–grader Jack Cuthbertson drove a horse–drawn wagon to collect the scrap and bring it to school. The metal was needed to make tanks and Liberty ships for the war.

The pile of broken tools and rusted farm equipment grew higher and higher. Before it was trucked away, Miss Shackelton took a picture of us standing in front of the scrap metal. We felt mighty proud.

One fall day an odd-looking bus without side windows pulled into the schoolyard. It was the bookmobile from the city library, bringing books to schools. We had very few books to read for fun in our school—or at home.

Most of us had never been on a bus of any kind. It was scary at first, stepping into the dark cavern of the bookmobile. Soon, though, a librarian helped us find treasures we could take home for a while.

On a blustery November day Dr. McGavern visited our school. The cloakroom became his office. One by one we entered to be examined. From a black leather bag he took a stethoscope to listen to our heartbeats, and tongue depressors to help see down our throats.

Our favorite visitor was Miss Meyers, the dental hygienist. With one foot she pushed a treadle that powered the device that cleaned everyone's teeth. Then she used a monkey hand puppet that held a tiny toothbrush to show the proper way to brush.

We began to learn songs for the Christmas concert, the one event all year that brought together the families scattered over the countryside. The concert was held on the night just before Christmas vacation. As the big night drew near, we made ringchains of colorful paper for our tree, and decorated the classroom walls and windows with our art.

Cars filled the schoolyard as our parents crowded into the classroom. Everyone, from first graders to eighth graders, had learned a poem, a story, a song, or some lines from a short play. A curtain made of old white bedsheets hung across the front of the room. We waited anxiously behind the curtain or in the cloakroom for our turn to perform.

My brother Gary and I sang "Silent Night." We were too scared to sing very loud. Still, the audience of moms and dads showered us with warm applause.

In February a blizzard struck. Wind swept across the fields and filled the roads with huge drifts of snow. Work crews struggled to clear the roads. School was closed. When it opened again, we walked on top of roadside snowbanks that plows had piled ten feet high.

Byron and Lucille Palmer had to hike two and a half miles each way. After the blizzard their mother hitched their bay horse, Mac, to a cutter and began driving them to school. That ended when Mac bolted and the sleigh tipped over, spilling everybody into the snow.

At lunchtime or recess we often played "Fox and Geese" in the snow. First we made a maze of trails and trampled the snow in two or three places where the geese could be safe from the fox for a while. Then one of us, the fox, would try to tag the others, the geese. During the chase, the fox and geese had to stay on the paths through the snow.

On the days the weather was too cold or rainy for outdoor play, we had spelling bees, or contests between two teams whose members raced to the blackboard to solve arithmetic problems. Sometimes Miss Shackelton played the piano for a game of musical chairs.

In the spring we played a game called "Anny Anny Over." We started with equal teams on the north and south sides of the school building. Yelling "Anny Anny over," one player threw the ball over the roof so that it rolled down the other side. The player who caught the ball would race around the school and tag someone on the other team. The tagged person had to join the players on the other side.

If the ball wasn't caught, someone yelled "Anny Anny over" and threw it over the roof toward the other team. At the end of recess, the team with the most players was the winner.

On warm spring days the school's heavy wooden door stood open. We could hear the chirps of house sparrows in the yard. Killdeer called "kill–dee, kill–dee" from the pasture.

The clock ticktocked from the wall. We longed for recess or lunchtime. Until then our only escape was performing a chore outdoors or going to the outhouse. Everyone's favorite chore was cleaning chalk erasers. We banged the erasers on the walls outdoors, sending up clouds of chalk dust. Girls daubed dust on their cheeks, pretending it was makeup.

When the school door stood open, Miss Shackelton could glance from her desk and see girls walk to and from their outhouse. Boys were out of Miss Shackelton's sight as they turned left and walked past the well pump, then along the path to their outhouse. Boys could linger outdoors longer. I looked across the pasture at the Hopper Hills and dreamed of exploring there.

My dream came true in May when Miss Shackelton led us on a nature walk. Carrying our lunches, we hiked across the pasture, leaped over little Hutchinson's creek, explored the wooded hills and reached Harloff's spring. Miss Shackelton pointed out the plants that she knew and encouraged us to pick wildflowers to take home to our mothers.

Along the creek the scent of mint filled the air as we stepped on a carpet of wild spearmint plants. The boys tried to catch frogs. Jack Cuthbertson looked for a snake to catch so he could tease the girls.

Lunch seemed to taste better outdoors when we sat in the spring sunshine by the lilac bush or by the well. Everyone brought lunch to school in a paper bag or metal lunchbox. Patricia Cutt, we agreed, had the best lunch of all. She often had dessert of chocolate cake with thick chocolate icing.

   We each had a Thermos of milk or drank water from the blue–and–white–striped crock that stood by the door. Fresh water from the well was poured into the crock each day, but it usually tasted warm and rusty.

Miss Shackelton always had lunch at her desk, listening to a radio for news of the war. The battles of World War II were far away, but the war touched all of our lives. Some of us had relatives fighting overseas. At home, supplies of sugar and gasoline were limited. Each family was given ration stamps that entitled them to buy some of these scarce supplies.

When Miss Shackelton announced an air–raid drill, we quickly left the building and lay down in the ditch across the road. It was fun, like an extra recess, because no airplanes ever raided our school or any other place in the United States.

The war ended in the summer. And that year, in June 1945, School 14 closed forever. In the fall we began to ride a bus to a big central school.

We never again set foot in our one room school. It was renovated as a home with indoor plumbing, so the outhouses were torn down. The elm tree that once served as third base in softball games was cut down. One owner moved the building into a new position in the old schoolyard. A cellar and more rooms were added to our schoolhouse.

Today it looks like an ordinary house. But the pasture is still there, and the wooded Hopper Hills still rise to the east. And some of us can still picture the school as it was. We remember the taste of the rusty well water and the smell of the dark oiled floors. And we can still hear the special clang of the bell that called us into our one room school.